To all the good readers
at St. Thomas More School —
Pig out on books!
Aliki Copeland
1991

PISTON AND THE PORKERS

b

PISTON AND THE PORKERS

By COLENE COPELAND
Illustrated By EDITH HARRISON

JORDAN VALLEY HERITAGE HOUSE

c

PISTON AND THE PORKERS

Library of Congress Catalog
Card number: 89-084652

ISBN: 0-939810-09-3 (Hardcover)
ISBN: 0-939810-10-7 (Paperback)

First edition

d

To my daughter, Deana.
"Don't take the cat to the pond."

e

Author's note
There are lots of stories yet to tell
about the goings on in the farrowing barn.
As long as you continue to request more
pig stories, I'll continue writing them.

f

CONTENTS

Mama was chatting with Little Prissy over her gate.

h

Chapter 1.

BAD NEWS

Papa sauntered uneasily through the front door of the farrowing barn. While he was out, he had heard bad news. He hated bringing home bad news and would put off telling Mama as long as possible.

Mama was chatting with Little Prissy over her gate. She loved spending time with her favorite little sow. Patsy and Penny, Prissy's daughters, who lived in the adjoining pen, listened.

Mama knew Papa had something on his mind. She knew Papa pretty well. He wasn't looking straight at her, which was a dead give away.

The hogs began making their usual noisy ruckus. Happy anxious sounds pealed the air. Papa's arrival meant it was supper time.

Mama asked, "How was the auction?" Maybe she could jog loose whatever it was he was not telling her.

1

"Didn't see anything I couldn't live without," he grinned. "I did see Glenn Greystone."

Whatever was bothering him had something to do with Glenn Greystone, Mama decided quickly.

"What's wrong, Papa?" she asked.

"After we get these hungry critters quieted down, I'll tell you some interesting news." He had a good excuse to delay the telling a bit longer.

The two of them worked quickly. Hog pellets were scooped into every feeder. Sows with pigs received a different ration than sows expecting pigs. Hogs just visiting were given a similar, yet different mixture. As they fed each sow, the sound changed from a noisy ruckus to satisfied munching sounds. No one in the world is more mesmerized by the taste of food, than a hog.

With the chore completed, they stood once again at the front of the barn by Little Prissy's pen.

"Now," Mama was curious, "What did Glenn Greystone have to say? Was it something about Piston?"

"You guessed it! It's about Piston. That ornery burro made the news again. Glenn told me about it, but I brought you a Salem newspaper so you can read it for yourself."

Theft of Burro Puzzles Police
Salem--- Idaho police still have no clues
in the theft Tuesday of a burro from a truck
stop near Boise. The burro, owned by local

residents Glenn and Alice Greystone, was one of the two being hauled by McMullen Brothers Trucking to a ranch in Montana.

The pet burros, fondly named Piston and Stinger, were both in the truck when the McMullen brothers stopped for lunch. When they returned less than 20 minutes later with fresh water and feed for the animals, the truck gate was still latched but Piston was missing. There was no sign of a break-in, nor was there any damage to the truck which would have occurred had the burro excaped by himself.

The McMullens, who have received many awards for their safe transport of animals, quickly notified the local police, who questioned truckers entering and exiting the truck stop, but none had noticed any activity in the vicinity of the McMullen truck. It was believed that by the time authorities arrived, the thief or thieves were gone from the area.

When they were notified of the theft by the Idaho police, the Greystones were puzzeled as to any motive, since the pet burros have no real value. They were adopted by the Greystones two years ago through a government program designed to save wild burros, and were being shipped to Greystone's brother's ranch in Montana so the animals would have more room to roam than the local small farm provides.

Piston is well-known here because of various destructive activities blamed on his dislike of confinement. His most recent escapade occurred during the severe storm which hit this area last week, when he did considerable damage to neighbor Bob Copeland's farrowing barn. Apparently frightened by the thunder and lightning, Piston escaped from his pasture and ended up at the Copelands, where he kicked down pens and injured several hogs, causing the premature delivery of a litter of pigs and the death of the sow, a valuable Landrace. When he was contacted this morning, Copeland reported that the baby pigs were hand-fed and all are doing fine.

The McMullens have continued their haul to Montana, where Stinger, the remaining burro, will be delivered to his future home.

"Oh, my! Piston stolen? Who would want him?" Mama asked.

"I don't know. But I'll tell you one thing, the joke is on the guy who stole him. Whoever has that burro on his hands is in for a whole peck of trouble!" Papa's was the voice of experience.

Word spread quickly through the farrowing barn. Immediately the sows chose up sides for and against Piston. It was about half one way and half the other.

Little Prissy had worked hard at trying to *hate* Piston. But she could not. It was not her nature to hate anyone. She sometimes thought she'd like to *dislike* him at least. After all, wasn't it this very same troublesome burro who had kicked her grandmother Mabel in the side, causing her death? But again she remembered Mabel's words as she lay dying. "It was only an accident. Please don't blame Piston. He was just frightened by the storm."

No matter what had happened in the past, Little Prissy would be the one heading the list of those most concerned for the welfare of Piston.

"Matt Ferrell was also at the auction." Papa said. "Every year about this time he asks me if I am taking any hogs to the State Fair, and every year I tell him no. He is so doggoned afraid of the competition. If I enter my hogs, he says, I'd beat him out of his blue ribbon for sure."

"That's a real compliment, Papa. Maybe you should enter a couple of the sows this year," Mama suggested.

"No thank you. I don't mind attending the fair a time or two every year. However, going there every day for eleven days, ---who would look after these girls and their babies?"

Mama knew he wouldn't enter. "Well, I plan to go two full days. One day to see what's there, and one day I'll take the grandkids to ride the rides."

"I believe those kids would ride rides all day, if they didn't run out of money." Papa remembered last year.

"Or get sick!" Mama also had recollections of the previous year.

Papa wisely said nothing. "No wonder the kids get sick," he thought. "Mama lets them eat anything they ask for. With hot dogs, cotton candy, curly fries, scones, Greek sandwiches, tacos, ice cream bars, popcorn, elephant ears, sno-cones, carameled apples and several flavors of soft drink, ---add to that, temperature in the 90's, and rides, one after the other, it's a

The calendar was properly marked.

wonder even one of them live through it. It's enough
to kill them all. But last year was the first time anyone had ever gotten sick, and then, only one. But kids
are kids. All of them are ready to go and do it all over

again." Papa chuckled to himself. He, too, loved to spoil the grandkids.

With the chores finished, Papa and Mama left the barn to the hogs, cats and an occasional wandering duck or chicken.

Although the summer had been a hot one, the past week, since the terrible storm, had been cloudy and cooler. Papa had had to turn on heat lamps for the sows with newborn pigs.

There were sixty 10' x 10' pens in the farrowing barn. A wide hallway down the center divided two rows of thirty pens.

At present, there were fifty-six sows in the barn, one to a pen, and one Hampshire gentleman hog, Charlie. Charlie was allowed to live in the barn because of his good disposition and gentle humor.

Another handsome male resided near the main barn. Big Red, a long, lean Duroc, had a small red barn all to himself, with access to the pasture. He didn't like being cooped up in the barn.

Red had an odd way of eating corn off the cob. Normally, a hog will leave an ear of corn on the ground, rolling it around as he eats all the kernals. Not Red! His corn never touched the ground. He would hold it in his mouth, spin it around, and nibble off every grain. When he spit out the cob, it was licked clean.

Supper was over. The barn was quiet. A full belly

in hogs as in humans, invites a nap. Now it was time
for the barn cats to do what they do best. Mice and
rats came through holes in the walls to feed on bits of
grain left by the hogs. The hogs were sleeping, but the
cats were wide awake, alert and ready. One after the
other a cat walked out the barn door, a catch in its
teeth. The pickings were plentiful.

Mabel's untimely death, the night of the storm
had brought many tears. Her orphaned pigs were bottle fed, and were placed in Prissy's pen for a few days.
But now they were back in the front pen so that Little Prissy could get some rest. After all, in a week's
time she would have babies of her own to contend
with and according to Little Prissy, "Pigs are pesky!"

Prissy was eager to talk to T.C. (Tom Cat) about
the disappearance of Piston. Since they'd heard the
news, her daughters, Patsy and Penny, in the adjoining pen, had talked of little else. But Prissy was tired,
her visit with T.C. would have to wait. She rearranged
her straw bed for comfort. Carefully, she lowered her
large frame and immediately fell asleep.

Suddenly, she was awakened by a grinning cat
who held something bloody and horrible looking in
his mouth.

Chapter 2.

FRIENDS FEELING HELPLESS

There stood Tom Cat with a half-eaten barn swallow in his teeth.

"Yuck! Get out of here with that bloody bird," Prissy demanded.

"It won't bite you, Porker," T.C. teased, after dropping his catch on Prissy's floor. "I'm saving the rest for Leeza. Have you seen her?"

"No. I can't believe you've lost track of your girl friend," Prissy smiled. "I'll bet she's not too far a—way."

Prissy was correct. Leeza, right on cue, jumped to the top boards of the pen. T.C. offered her his catch. Without a word, she jumped down to pick up the bird and was quickly out of sight.

Prissy thought this beautiful white Angora looked pretty silly with an ugly, half-eaten bird hanging from her mouth. She began to laugh. The floor vibrated

9

from her large body. Tom Cat took pleasure in anything that made his "Porker" happy. Prissy had had a lot of sadness in her life. T.C. liked being with her and watching out for her. Theirs was a special friendship that began when Prissy was born.

"Did you hear the news about Piston?" Prissy asked.

"No. What about him? I've been in the timber, hunting where it's cooler. Caught a bird, ---no sweat!" he bragged.

The Tom Cat listened to all the details of Piston's disappearance, just as Prissy had heard them from Mama and Papa.

"I wish there was something we could do," the cat announced. "But Boise, Idaho, must be a long way from here."

"It is." Prissy answered.

Tom Cat pondered Little Prissy's words for a moment.

"How do you know?" he asked.

"My mother, Priscilla, told me. I know that Idaho is east of Oregon and Montana is beyond Idaho. She learned a lot from watching television."

"Well, what do you know!" T.C. thought. "Not long ago when I returned home from California, Prissy wouldn't dare talk like this about Priscilla, who used to live in the farm house. She was afraid the sows would make fun of her, or think she was bragging. Would you listen to her now?" Tom Cat was happy to see the change.

"It happened so far away, T.C. This time there's nothing we can do." The tired little sow drifted off to sleep again.

Leeza sat in the hallway grooming her face. The bird was no more. T.C. shot up to the rafters above Little Prissy's pen. Leeza was not far behind.

Later in the evening, Papa and Maggie, the Springer Spaniel, came back to the barn for a bedtime check. A young sow was due to farrow in a day or two. Sometimes a first litter of pigs arrives early. But after a careful examination, Papa knew there would be no baby pigs tonight.

Suddenly, Mabel's pigs became upset about something. They began to squeal, shrill, piercing sounds jolting the evening calm. Hog city came to its feet!

Papa and Maggie hurried over to the pen. Maggie began to bark at something. She wanted inside. She saw the intruder before Papa did. A snake had invaded the pen. It was a red racer, his body strung out about 18 inches across the floor.

The pigs were in no immediate danger, but they were frightened all the same. If their mother had been present, she would have bitten the snake and shook it to death. But Mabel's babies had no mother. They were orphans.

As soon as he opened the gate, Maggie darted in.

Papa put on his gloves. His intentions were to pick up the snake on a stick and throw it out in the pasture. But as soon as he opened the gate, Maggie darted in. *Now* the pigs were really upset. The pigs were squealing, the dog was barking and every hog in the place was grunting and snorting loudly. The racket really played havoc with Papa's nervous system.

Quickly he shut the hallway doors. The sows were so excited they might push down the gates to their pens. Chasing pigs all over the farm was not his idea of a good time.

Maggie had the snake in her mouth. She ran from the barn, with Papa in pursuit. As soon as they got outside, Maggie dropped the frightened snake on the ground and began to play with it with her foot. Now that her mouth was empty, she again began to bark. The snake was very much alive. Quickly, Papa shoved a flat stick under it and was about to give it a sling, when Maggie decided she wasn't finished with it. She yanked it off the stick.

Papa lost his temper. He waved the stick at Maggie as though he was going to hit her. Although he had never laid a hand on the dog, the gesture did the trick. Maggie dropped the snake, and stood back until Papa slung it out into the pasture. But as soon as it left his hand she took off after it. Papa yelled for her to come back. He grabbed her by the collar and put her in the pickup truck to settle down.

What a fuss! Settling down, for the hogs, for Maggie, and for Papa, took a few minutes.

Little Prissy wished she could have been more help to Mabel's pigs. At first, Papa had left her gate and the gate to the orphans' pen open. She popped in and out to check on them. Now that wasn't possible. The pigs were growing rapidly on their diet of hand-feeding, starter pellets and water. Their gate had to be closed so they couldn't escape. But Prissy's gate remained open. It was the only open gate in the farrowing barn. Little Prissy was a privileged porker!

Prissy hoped there would be no more disturbances in the barn tonight. When all was calm, her thoughts went to Piston. She hoped with all her heart that he was safe.

Chapter 3.

BAD LUCK

L ittle Prissy would really have worried if she had known what a mess of trouble Piston was in. And for once, he had done nothing wrong.

But there he stood, just about as miserable and unhappy as a fellow could be. He was tied to the back side of a stinking horse trailer, with a heavy rusty chain. At first, he had been tied with a rope. But in no time at all he had the cords chewed in two and took off running.

His freedom lasted the distance of a few yards. He got all tangled up in a large pile of rope and canvas being unloaded from a company truck. Like it or not, he was suddenly involved with a carnival.

Victor Rossi wasted no time in taking advantage of Piston's unfortunate situation. He rushed forth, heaving a strong net over his stolen property. Piston.

The burro felt trapped and humiliated as he was pulled back to the spot from whence he had fled.

Following that one and only escape, Rossi had replaced the rope with a length of heavy, rusty chain.

Victor Rossi was en route from Salt Lake City, Utah, to Spokane, Washington, traveling with the Vagabond Carnival caravan. When he drove into a truck stop in Boise, Idaho, his evil eyes immediately caught sight of two healthy looking burros in a parked truck. No one was around. Quickly, Rossi backed his truck up to the McMullen's rig. He opened the back gates to both vehicles. A rope went around Piston's neck. In a matter of seconds Rossi had managed to perform the maneuver, most skillfully.

The burro was completely taken by surprise. It was probably the first time in his life he had been outsmarted.

"If only I had known what I was getting in to," he moaned to himself, "I would have put up more of a battle."

Rossi wanted both burros as badly as he ever wanted anything in his life. Stinger ran to the front of the McMullen truck, away from the gate, and began to bray. Rossi didn't want to get caught. He became nervous. One, would have to do. Quickly closing and latching the truck gates, he wheeled onto the highway and headed west.

"After all," he told himself, "it will be hard

enough to steal enough food for one of these mutts." The man had been a cowardly thief, all of his 47 years.

Rossi was of medium height, with dark skin and eyes to match. Except for a gigantic bulge of a belly, he was squarely built. His hair and beard were dark, curly and matted. One feature about this man was outstanding. He smelled awful. God only knows how long it had been since he had a bath, or put on clean clothes.

Piston could not ignore the odor. When Rossi came near him, it was sickening.

Now, a week later, Piston was tired and hungry. During that time, the work had never ended, yet feeding time seldom began. It was not surprising that he had lost several pounds.

Victor Rossi's duties for Vagabond Carnival Company were to load and unload trucks and to move equipment from one place to another. This week, Piston's back had carried the loads. The last burro Rossi owned was so cruelly treated that one day the poor, half-starved beast dropped dead on the job.

The big tent had been the hardest to move. Piston had pulled as much as his weary body would allow. Suddenly, he had stepped on a slick spot on the ground. He lost his footing; down he went, both front knees hitting cement. Victor grabbed a long leather bull whip out of a near-by truck. He cracked it hard

God only knows how long it had been since Victor Rossi had had a bath or put on clean clothes.

across Piston's back, ripping the hide.

A frail looking, little midget ran up to Rossi, begging him to stop being so cruel to the little burro.

"What ya gonna do about it, you little squirt?" Victor growled, "You gonna hurt me, you think? Now git! Before I take this leather to *your* back."

"You'd better not mistreat that animal again!" the midget yelled, when he had retreated to a safe distance.

Rossi examined the bull whip. Nice! Instead of returning it to its owner, he placed it in his own truck.

But the cruelty never ended, nor did the heavy labor.

Now, what Piston wanted more than anything else, was just a clean drink of water. His water bucket smelled so foully that it was not pleasant to drink from it. In fact, the entire area around Victor Rossi's trailer was dirty and foul smelling.

While the rest of the carnival seemed fairly clean, there was definitely nothing clean about Victor Rossi.

Most of the time when the fair grounds were opened to the public, Piston was chained for the full twelve hours. His labor began when the grounds were shut down for the night.

At first, Piston tried to enjoy the carnival as he stood tied. He listened to the music and the laughter of the children as they rode the rides. There were always screams! Lots of screams!

"Why do they ride on rides they are afraid of?" he asked himself. "That would be silly."

Now all he could think about was getting away from this place.

"There has to be a way," he told himself, over and over. But Rossi kept him chained tightly. An escape would not be easy. He would not give up hope. Perhaps when the carnival moved again, from Spokane to Seattle, opportunity might present itself. It would be a long ride. First, he needed rest and food. In his present condition, running very fast was out of the question. Yes, first he would rest and then, ---he would use his strength, break out of the truck and run for cover.

Piston knew he must escape. He had already heard what happened to Rossi's last burro. He hoped and prayed he would be able to get away. But when the time came, if it ever did, would he be strong enough to flee?

Chapter 4.

A DAY AT THE FARM

The four grandkids were spending a few days on the farm with Papa and Mama. Christina and Sara liked it better when they visited without their brothers. But this time, Shawn and little Steven wanted to have their turn.

Steven watched as Shuffles and her baby ducks paddled across the pond. He kept calling to them as they swam faster in the opposite direction. Perhaps the duck family wasn't sure whether this little rascal could be trusted.

Shawn headed for the timber at the rear of the farm. Exploring this sixty acres of wooded area would be any boy's dream. There were wild animals, all kinds of birds, and a rippling stream that flowed year round. But first, he wanted to visit the pet cemetery to see where Mabel had recently been laid to

21

rest. The loveliest spot in the timber had been select-
ed for a burial ground. Giant Oregon pines protected
it on the left, and on the right rose a stately Chinese
elm tree. Buried here, in addition to Mabel, were
other favorite sows, such as Hotsie and Priscilla, Little
Prissy's mother, and other well-loved household pets.
Each grave was marked with a large, flat river stone.
Shawn, rowdy and mischievous as any normal boy,
secretly loved the serenity of the pet cemetery.

The girls were glad their brothers had found
things to occupy their time. As usual, Christina and
Sara ran down the center aisle of the farrowing barn
"Helloing" the hogs. There were new pigs to look at
and "ooh" and "aw" over. They helped Mama bottle
feed Mabel's pigs. Already, her babies were pigging
out on solid little pig pellets, but they never, ever
refused the bottles of milk. The girls still had their
favorites. Crackerbelle liked for Sara to carry her
around, while Thunder, Christina's pick of the litter,
would rather follow along behind her. The faster she
walked, the louder Thunder grunted.

"Has Piston been found, grandma?" Christina
asked.

"We haven't heard a word honey. Papa has checked with the Greystones, several times," Mama said
sadly. "They feel pretty badly. In fact, they feel responsible! But of course they aren't to blame.

Crackerbelle liked for Sara to carry her around, while Thunder, Christina's pick of the litter, would rather follow along behind.

"Strange about Piston. It's almost as if a great whirlwind came along and sucked him up."

"And was never seen or heard from again," Sara added.

"I hope you're wrong, Sara. Papa hasn't forgiven Piston for all the trouble he caused here." Mama looked at Little Prissy. "I keep trying to tell myself that it was his fear of the storm that made him do what he did." Prissy understood.

Papa came in carrying a bale of straw.

"Are you girls saving your money for the State Fair?" he asked.

Christina was happy that her grandpa remembered the fair. Attending the fair with Grandma and Grandpa was a family tradition, almost as good as Christmas, and costing about the same.

"Of course we are, Grandpa," she answered.

"How would the two of you like to do some special jobs today and earn some money?" he asked.

"The stuff we do here is fun, Grandpa. It's never like work. You always say you do things for us, for love, so let us help you for love too," Christina told him.

"Well, that's nice honey, but I just thought --?

Sara interupted, "But those rides at the fair do cost a lot of money, Christy," she giggled.

"They sure do, Sara," Mama added.

"I've tacked a long list of things-to-do on the

The girls continued doing the jobs on Papa's list.

storage room door. Pick something you know how to do. When it's done, cross it off the list. Let's see how quickly all of us can get *my* work done, before the old thermometer pops its cork," he grinned.

The girls checked the list. Sara threw all the baby bottles in a basket and skipped across the orchard to the house with them. She cleaned them all for the next feeding. Mama was at the kitchen table, planning something special for lunch.

Papa loaded bags of feed on the wheelbarrow for Christina. Down the hallway she went, filling all the feed storage barrels. Leeza was taking a nap on the lid of one of the barrels. The cat opened her eyes, but did not move as Christina lifted the lid and the cat to the ground. When the container was filled, she replaced them. Leeza went back to sleep.

After Papa had sprayed and disinfected all the empty pens, he brought in fresh cedar shavings for the floors. There had never been any hog diseases in his barns.

The girls cleaned and filled all the water tubs. Christina did all the pens on the left and Sara the ones on the right.

Papa oiled and brushed about a dozen sows. The oil was plain old cheap motor oil, but it left their coats soft and shiny.

The vet stopped by to check the cast on Rosie's leg. Rosie had received multiple cuts and bruises as well as a broken leg, the night Piston kicked the barn apart during the storm. Heavy timbers, several of them, had fallen on the sow. She would have died had it not been for Little Prissy and Tom Cat who ran to the house for help.

The sow was healing, but she would still be wearing the cast when her pigs were due in a couple of weeks.

Five year old Steven learned that Rosie would have some baby pigs soon. Steven looked at Rosie's cast.

"Do pigs always look like their mothers?" he asked Christina.

"Most of the time, darling," she answered.

Steven was curious. "Then will her babies be born with casts on their legs?" He was so serious, no one dared to laugh.

"Probably not, darling," Christina answered, trying hard to keep a straight face. Those two had always called each other "darling".

It was noon when Mama and Steven walked into the barn carrying a picnic basket and a jug.

"Let's eat!" Steven hollered.

"Is the food for us or for the hogs, Grandma?" Sara asked.

"It's fried chicken! Does that tell you anything?" Mama laughed.

When Papa heard 'fried chicken', he came running. "Shawn's in the timber; let's join him out there for lunch."

Hearing no complaints, he hitched the small trailer to the tractor. Everybody crowded in, even Maggie, the dog.

"Let me drive?" Christina begged.

"Well ---come on!" Papa agreed.

Christina got in the tractor seat. Papa stood behind on the drawbar and gave instructions. She started up with a jerk.

"Watch it, Christy!" Sara shouted, "You're gonna throw us out of this trailer!"

Maggie jumped out, not trusting Christina's driving, and followed along behind.

"I think you're smarter than we are, Maggie." Sara said to the dog.

"Is my darling going to wreck us?" little Steven asked. He had always trusted his "darling", but this time he was showing doubt. Christina and Steven, the oldest and the youngest, had a special bond.

"No Steven! She is just learning how to drive. Everything will be O.K.," Mama assured him. Steven was not convinced. He didn't smile again until they were parked, sitting on a fallen pine tree, and he was handed a chicken leg. Then he smiled.

Papa yelled for Shawn. But Shawn did not come.

Chapter 5.

EARNING MONEY FOR THE FAIR

Shawn didn't show up until the whole family loudly threatened to eat his pieces of fried chicken. Only then did he come running. He was wet, dirty, his pants were torn, but he had a smile on his face and was anxious to return to whatever it was he'd been doing. While he scarfed down his food, he gave a full report.

First, he had visited the cemetery and had placed some wildflowers on the graves, a bouquet each for Hotsie, Priscilla, Mitzi and Mabel.

Then, he had spotted several animal tracks made by deer, squirrel, rabbit and fox. When he was called for lunch, he had been busy making a small temporary dam in Mill Creek to aid with the trout fishing he intended to do that afternoon. His adventures sounded so exciting that Steven decided to join him for the rest of the day.

29

After lunch, the boys took off running through the woods. The rest of the family paid a visit to the cemetery before returning to work. Such a pretty spot.

"Good friends, all," Papa said, looking at the stones.

"I wonder about Piston. Is he dead or alive?" Mama asked, thoughtfully. "I know you don't care much for him, Papa, after all the trouble he caused us, but Mabel didn't hold it against him."

Papa looked at her, "Gosh sakes, dear! Are you trying to tell me that you could talk to Mabel too?"

"No, just Little Prissy. She told me about Mabel's feelings," she answered plainly. Mama never seemed to realize that other people might think it was a bit strange to carry on a conversation with a hog.

Christina and Sara were thoroughly enjoying *this* conversation. They weren't saying a word. Papa didn't want anybody to know about the unusual talent his wife had. On the other hand, he never doubted it for a minute. First, it was Priscilla she understood, and now Priscilla's daughter, Little Prissy.

There was much work yet to do in the barn. First, Papa had a look at Tilly, the young sow he had checked the previous evening. She was in labor. Pigs would begin to be born in about two hours.

Preparations began for the arrival of the litter.

The afternoon was heating up. Sara turned on an overhead fan. It began to make a racket, which scared Tilly. A substitute was found, a smaller, quiet fan, to use until Papa could crawl up above and fix the big one. A bucket of ice water was near by for cold towels, if needed. All of this was being done for Tilly and her comfort.

The girls continued doing the jobs on Papa's list and marking them off: Hose down the hallway to settle the dust. Sweep down any dust or webs, overhead. Put empty feed sacks in the big metal containter. Add more oil to the hog squirter bottles. Clean the hogs' combs and brushes with the special cleaning gunk. Put fresh bedding straw in front of pens where there was none left.

Christina and Sara took only one break, well earned. Hot and thirsty, they poured two large paper cups of lemonade from the jug, and headed for the grassy knoll under the great, broad, pine tree in the pasture.

Victoria, the old white Landrace, was snoozing there. The girls knew Victoria wouldn't mind sharing her shade.

Mama took time out to make an angel food cake at Christina's request. When the girls and Mama returned to the barn, Tilly had three pigs. And soon there were twelve.

"Where are Tom Cat and Leeza today?" Sara

asked. "They are usually with Prissy, or underfoot."

"Leeza was on top of the feed barrel this morning. She just laid there while I moved her, with the lid." Christina recalled. "She is all right, isn't she, Grandma?"

Mama didn't answer. She looked toward Prissy and then back at Christina but said nothing.

Mama knew that Leeza had been spending a lot of time in Rosie's pen. That was strange. No one ever liked Rosie enough to visit. The sow was never very good company. Perhaps Leeza saw some good in her. Mama wondered what they talked about.

For now at least, Mama did not want to be the one to tell this to Little Prissy. She knew Prissy and Rosie were not good friends. Since Rosie was so hateful to Prissy, that made Rosie a natural enemy of Tom Cat. He had loved Little Prissy since the day she was born. Indeed, he had been her first friend.

What would T.C. do when he found out that Leeza was visiting with his enemy?

St. Thomas More School
3521 S.W. Patton Road
Portland, Or 97221

Chapter 6.

PRISSY'S BIG DAY

Today was Little Prissy's day, once again, to become a mother. This date had been circled on the calendar for a long time. Mama gave her favorite little sow much more attention than was necessary. She wouldn't be outside that pen more than ten minutes at a time until every pig was born and doing fine.

"I owe it to Priscilla," she told Papa, "And to Prissy."

The day was quite warm, about 80 degrees, but not a scorcher. Prissy was off her food. That was normal. She had not begin nesting, so delivery time was several hours away. By then, the day would be cooler.

"Conditions should be just about perfect," Mama told Prissy, who was not nearly as concerned as Mama.

34

Also keeping Prissy company were her daughters, next door. They chatted through the boards dividing their pens. Mama was pleased by the fact that she was understanding a lot of what the girls were saying. First Priscilla, then Little Prissy, and now Patsy and Penny!

"Won't Papa be surprised?" she thought. Someone should tell her, "No! Papa will not be surprised."

Rosie was the topic of conversation. Why had she been so quiet lately, no nasty remarks, no rumors? They tried to guess what was going on.

"Let's leave well enough alone, girls!" Prissy said. "Just wait until that cast comes off," she laughed. "She'll get back to doing what she does best." Rosie was an expert at gossipping and putting her peers in awkward positions.

"I don't like that sow," Patsy announced loudly. "I don't care if she does have a broken leg! She never, ever thanked you, mother, for going for help when she was lying under that pile of timber, all busted and bleeding. She would have died!"

"Don't let it trouble you, child," Prissy counceled. "It doesn't matter. I did it to be kind and because I was truly concerned about her."

Penny thought she was hearing things!

"Mother, you should have heard yourself! You said that just like Mabel would have when you called Patsy, 'child'. Remember how she called you 'child'?"

"Of course, I remember," Prissy answered sadly. There was a tear in her eye. "She called Priscilla 'child' too," she said wearily, before dropping off to sleep. The conversation ended there.

That evening, in the course of two hours, the little sow had sixteen perfect baby pigs.

Papa could not stop smiling. Pleased? You bet. Not a runt in the bunch. All the babies were rusty red, like their mother.

Compliments poured from Papa.

"When Hotsie died, I thought we'd seen the last of splendid, flawless litters like this one. These guys are in every way the picture of perfection." He knelt down by Prissy's head.

"Little gal, *you* are a wonder."

Prissy thanked him for all the kind words, but he did not understand. He took them for happy grunts.

Mama was there. "She's thanking you, Papa, for the kind words."

Papa grinned, "If you say so," he said. "I want to invite Matt Ferrell to come to see these beauties." He hurried to the phone in the storage room to call his friend. He didn't stop to consider what time of night it was. Matt Ferrell had probably gone to bed.

"He's gone to brag on you, Prissy." Mama patted the sow's head and one by one, gently lifted each baby to give it one more hug before she slipped quietly out the gate. She needed rest and so did the sow.

Tom Cat jumped down from his perch in the rafters. Leeza followed.

"I say there, Little Porker, looks like you might be needing a baby sitter," he grinned a devilish grin.

"Wouldn't my mother be proud, T.C., if she could see my new family?" Prissy asked longingly.

"Yeah! Indeed! How do you know she hasn't seen them already?" the cat asked. He was remembering a vision he had had before the storm, in which Hotsie and Priscilla had warned of coming danger.

"May be." Prissy agreed. "I often feel like Priscilla is near; Mabel, too. I can't explain it. I never see them. I know they died. But sometimes, well ---I just feel it."

Leeza rubbed up to the sleeping newborns. She loved the farm and all the animals, but the lovely cat had a burdensome secret. She had told no one, not even T.C. She worried constantly, but she kept it to herself. She wanted to tell the Tom Cat; she had come close, but she was afraid.

"Why can't I be more like him?" Leeza wondered. "He talks easily about everything. His life is an open book." But, thoughtful, kind Leeza was too quiet and shy to share her worries, even with her beloved T.C.

Often she thought about the Killians, who had once owned her. She remembers things better forgotten. Three times she had had kittens and three times the Killians sold them all to add money to their "petty cat cash". The money was spent for their pleasure, on things like trips and trinkets.

Leeza never knew what happened to her kittens. Never once did she get to keep one.

It had taken much courage to leave the Killians. At least they fed her and gave her a home. But they never talked to her or petted her like most people do their pets. Poor Leeza was a money maker for the Killians and that was all there was to it.

Had it not been for T.C., Leeza would still be with the Killians, making them money. She and the Tom Cat had met when T.C. hitchhiked a ride on the Killian travel trailer. He was on his way home from a trip to California and was anxious to get there in a hurry. She envied his freedom, and, he was such a handsome fellow. She asked him what roads he would take to get to the farm. Leeza listened carefully and stored the information away in her brain. After he headed across the fields for home, she thought about him all the time. Finally, one day, she mustered up her nerve. She watched for an opportunity to slip out of the house.

Leeza had been happy here on the farm. Everyone made her welcome. Papa and Mama and all the kids were always picking her up and telling her how beautiful she was. She knew they really cared about her. But now, with this problem, what could she do?

Would she have to leave again, go where no one knew her? And if so, where would she go?

Chapter 7.

MUCH DISTRESS AND LITTLE COMFORT

Vagabond Carnival Company moved to Seattle. Victor Rossi and Piston moved along with them.

Sadly enough, Piston was still on the truck. There had been absolutely no chance for escape. After all his planning, not even one opportunity presented itself.

Rossi was a brutal man. Suspecting that Piston might try to break away en route, he packed the poor fellow into the tightest quarters he could. Then, all four feet were fastened together with a chain. The only way Piston could lie down was to fall down. Once he was down, there was no getting up.

After traveling 280 miles from Spokane to Seattle in the rough-riding old truck, Piston had cuts and bruises from the chains. When he arrived, he was one sick burro. There was blood on the floor where the

40

chains had cut into his ankles. He had lain in the blood and now the dried blood was caked on his body.

There had been only one stop during the seven hour trip. In Ellenburg, Washington, the caravan pulled in for gas and lunch.

In Ellenburg, the midget waited for a chance. As soon as Rossi was out of sight, he brought Piston a drink of water. He knew that Rossi wouldn't do it. Twice in the past week the midget had brought food, clean water, and salve for the cuts.

Truthfully, the midget was afraid of Rossi. He

The midget, bringing water to Piston.

knew the man well. His life would be in danger if he were caught interfering, but he had a fond affection and sympathy for the burro. He felt that he must take the risk, and slip in and help when circumstances allowed it.

"Doesn't anyone except this poor, scared, little midget fellow care about the likes of me?" Piston asked himself. "Surely I've been noticed! Will help ever come?"

The back door of the truck flew open. There stood Rossi, hands on his hips, making an arrogant, chortling sound.

About the same time, John Patton walked behind the truck. John was a large, muscular man, a driver for one of the carnival rigs. Evidently, he was not a-ware that the vehicle belonged to one Victor Rossi, or that Rossi was the one responsible for the condition of the burro.

"What's the matter here? What's the problem with that poor beast?" he asked, looking over Rossi's shoulder.

Rossi did not answer.

"Look at this poor animal! What kind of an ig-norant jerk would chain an animal like that?" John asked angrily.

Again, Rossi did not answer.

John Patton lost no time. Quickly, he went to work removing the rusty old chains coiled tightly around Piston's legs.

"Come on, man, let's get him out of there," he said to Rossi. Rossi gave assistance, but said nothing.

Piston saw a little ray of hope. He welcomed the kind treatment from this large, gentle man.

Piston was a pitiful mess. He was dirty, bruised and bleeding, and he was hungry. The poor animal was totally humiliated. Rossi had not only stolen him, but had stripped him of his dignity.

When the chains were removed, Piston could bare-ly stand up. John turned on a near-by water hose. He was hosing down the animal when the midget sudden-ly appreared. He stretched forth his hand to John. In it was a can of healing salve.

"Here, use this on the cuts," he said.

John looked at this strange little man as if to say, "Where did you come from?" He was grateful for the midget's help.

Piston was also grateful for any consideration that came his way, for lately very little had.

The midget stood some distance away and watch-ed. Perhaps if he waited, he might have a chance to talk alone with this man who had taken an interest in the burro. Maybe somehow, the two of them could get the animal away from Rossi. What would John Patton do if he knew Rossi was responsible for this? But he thought Rossi was a carnival worker who, like John, just happened along. John was beginning to think the man was deaf and dumb.

Rossi disappeared for a few minutes. He returned with a few ears of corn and some hay.

Piston was surprised. "I wonder who he managed to steal that from?" he thought. Piston knew that every mouth full of food he'd been given was stolen, either from the agricultural buildings or one of the many food stands. He did not like the idea of eating stolen food. But for Piston, it was either eat it or starve to death.

A young lady in a red dress and high heel shoes to match came toward them, stepping carefully over the gravel. She waved her arms, trying to attract John's attention.

"Are you John Patton?" she asked.

"That's me!" he answered, handing the well-used can of salve back to the midget.

"There's an emergency phone call for you, John, in the ticket office."

"For me?" He acted surprised.

"Yes," she said. "It sounds rather urgent."

"I'll be right there. Thank you." John gave Piston a hug around the neck and a pat on the rump. He turned and hurried to the ticket office.

Piston's poor heart sank. "Please, please come back and be my friend," he cried as John walked away from him.

It was not to be. The phone call was an urgent

summons to an eagerly-awaited new job in another
state. John was a kind man, and he had done the best
he could for the unfortunate burro during their brief
encounter. Thoughts of his new opportunities crowded the burro from his mind as he boarded a plane for
a new career. He had no way of knowing the hopes he
had kindled in the hearts of Piston and the midget.
They believed they had found someone else who
cared, someone large and muscular. Someone Rossi
was afraid to cross. But John did not return, and with
no one watching, Rossi shoved Piston back into the
truck and replaced the cruel leg chains, then gave
Piston a vicious kick.

"You almost got me into trouble," he muttered.

Things were back to normal. The burro was either
weighted down with heavy loads or dragging them behind him. The cargo was always far too great for an
animal of his size. When it was time to stop work for
the day, conditions improved very little. That cussed
heavy chain would be hooked to the one already
around his neck. The chain was short. He could either
stand up, in one spot, or lie down on the filthy cement until it was time to go to work again.

Most days there was little or no food. Occasion-
ally, the midget would try to help. Once he threw an
ear of corn over to Piston. It fell short. Piston tried to
reach it, but the chain wasn't long enough. The kind-
hearted little man could not bear watching the burro

More heavy cargo to be loaded on Piston's back.

struggling, using all his strength, to reach the food. Quickly, he ran near, and kicked the corn within reach. Rossi spied him, and yelled threats of violence. The midget was terrified.

"How long?" Piston moaned. "How long can I live?" He lay down on the dirty ground and wept, bitterly.

Chapter 8.

FRIENDS AND ENEMIES

The farrowing barn was bustling with activity. Several of Papa's friends had come by to see Little Prissy's litter. Each of the sixteen pigs weighed about three and a half pounds. They were strong and healthy. Since Papa was unable to come up with a word wonderful enough to describe this litter of pigs, he made up one of his own. His friends thought he was a very smart fellow because he used this big word. The word was "katureferpeango" (ka-tour'-ee-fer'-pee-ango). Papa bragged, "It's not e-nough to say these pigs are wonderful and great. They are katureferpeango." Which meant, according to Papa, "too gorgeous for words". Papa had a good time teaching everybody to say his word.

Little Prissy was not used to all the attention. She permitted any of the family to pick up her pigs, but not outsiders. She chased them right out of her pen.

Which meant, according to Papa, "too gorgeous for words."

"Thought all you hogs were friendly," Ira Cook commented to Papa.

"They are, Ira. But not to strangers." Papa answered. He pointed to Mama and Steven going in and out of the pens.

"I see what you mean," Ira acknowledged.

Ira tried to buy several sows from Papa, including Patsy and Penny. Papa laughed and shook his head. Ira kept raising the offer.

"Not for sale at any price," Papa told him. "Besides, those girls are Little Prissy's daughters."

"Well, ---they *are* beauties," Ira conceded.

"I know. That's why I kept them," Papa smiled.

Papa liked showing off all his hogs. Beauties, every one. They were clean, healthy and content. The barn was spotless and smelled of cedar shavings and fresh wheat straw. Papa worked hard and was proud of all his animals. Vacations were planned for months ahead. Whoever was left in charge was trained and retrained. Each detail had to be worked out to Papa's particular way of doing things. It wasn't easy for him to walk away and leave his hogs in someone else's care, even for a few days.

Peaches, normally a docile sow, was quite upset. She hated visitors in the barn. It was a good thing the men couldn't understand what she was saying about them. It was neither polite nor complimentary.

Finally, she became so annoyed that she took

matters into her own hands. She jumped up, her front feet coming to rest on the top boards of her pen, and unleashed her temper in the direction of the strangers.

Everybody got a tongue lashing, except Papa. Her feet came down so hard on the top board that somehow the bottom board came loose.

Splash, her water-loving son, noticed immediately. Aw haw! An escape route. Out he went, followed by all his brothers and sisters. They took off racing down the center hallway, not knowing where they were going and caring less.

Papa shut the lower front barn door. Then he ran around the side of the barn to shut the doors at the far end. When he showed up at the back door, his unexpected presence startled the pigs. They spun around and ran in the opposite direction for a few feet, then stopped to look back at Papa. He could have herded them back into their pen, but if he didn't repair it first, they would escape again.

Now that they were contained within the hallway, he'd let them visit with other pigs for a while. Already, happy little noses were sticking through the boards here and there to greet them.

Splash found the little red tub of water about half way down the hall, drinking water for dogs, cats, ducks, chickens or any other critter who happened to be passing through the barn. Splash didn't care whose water it was. It was a hot day, and water was water, where ever one may find it. In he jumped! Splash! That's how he got his name in the first place.

"There he goes again!" Mama laughed.

"Why does that pig do that, Grandma?" Steven asked.

"Because he loves water, honey, just like you do," Mama answered.

"Why doesn't Grandpa build him a swimming pool?" Steven asked, sincerely.

"Oh, Steven, please don't mention that to your grandpa. He might be tempted. Our hogs are already the most pampered hogs in the county."

The visitors left.

Papa repaired the loose boards. Peaches once again settled down. Her pigs were ready to go home after their nice taste of freedom. Even Splash hurried back to his mother.

As soon as Papa and Mama and Steven had gone, Rosie began to complain.

"Well, Prissy, I hope you're satisfied! You certainly got enough attention! I'm the one suffering because of that stupid burro. I'm the one with the bruises and a broken leg. But did anyone pay any attention to me? Did I get any sympathy? No! Not one little bit!"

Patsy and Penny sprang to their feet, ready to take on Rosie in their mother's behalf.

Rosie's harsh words caused an alarm to sound in the Tom Cat's head. Awaking from a peaceful nap, he bounded down from the rafters. In seconds he stood with Patsy and Penny to match wits with Rosie.

Little Prissy's allies still carried a grudge against gossipy Rosie. Not long ago, Rosie had started a rumor that Mama and Papa were going to sell Prissy because she reminded them too much of Priscilla. Prissy knew that Mama and Papa were still grieving over Priscilla's death, so it was easy to believe that the rumor might be true. Rosie's lie caused Prissy a great deal of sadness and concern, until she learned that Rosie was just being Rosie, causing trouble.

T.C. let fly with what he deemed to be a terrific insult.

"Rosie, jealousy makes your nostrils flare and look funny."

Patsy and Penny enjoyed listening to his verbal abuse. Leeza heard him and was sorely confused. Rosie's hurtful rumor had been passed around the barn before Leeza arrived there, so she didn't understand T.C.'s dislike. Leeza felt sorry for Rosie because of her cast, and visited with her each day to cheer her up. Leeza, like Little Prissy, saw good in everyone.

Penny wouldn't miss a chance to slam Rosie.

"You have no right, no right at all, to be unkind to our mother," she said. "Besides, she earned all the attention she got, and more."

Slowly, Little Prissy got up from her straw.

"Tell her off, Porker!" T.C. coaxed.

But this kind little sow had no intention of telling anybody off, not even Rosie. True, Rosie's lies had caused Prissy many sleepless nights. Rosie delighted in making Prissy miserable, for some reason. And it was not only Prissy. She took great pleasure in tormenting all the sows. No one knew why.

"You'll get attention when your babies arrive, Rosie," Little Prissy said sweetly.

"Not like you do," Rosie responded, which in itself was quite remarkable. Rosie had never, ever responded to Little Prissy.

"My mother told me about the night your brothers and sisters were born," Prissy recalled. "She said it was the coldest night of the year. She said that even though Papa checked on your mother several times, she fooled him and had her family during the night. And even with the heat lamps on to beckon the newborn babies, they went to a far corner, and the poor little things froze to death." Prissy was sad about that. Even Prissy's allies were sorry for Rosie. "Wasn't it lucky for you and Posey, your sister, that Mama and Papa arrived when they did? You two were just about to be born. They stuck you under the heat lamp immediately."

This time, Rosie did not respond.

"I wish I had a sister, Rosie. It must be nice. All

of my brothers and sisters died. I see how Patsy and Penny enjoy each other's company," Prissy continued.

Tom Cat had listened patiently, a difficult task for this mouthy critter.

"Give it up, Porker! She doesn't deserve the kind words, nor your time. And speaking of time, it's my opinion, yours is being wasted on that piece of lard."

"Please don't be so unkind, T.C.; Rosie hasn't been well. That cast on her leg can't be a comfortable thing to be burdened with," Prissy continued to protect her enemy.

The Tom Cat gave up. As hard as they tried, he and the girls could not stir any anger from Prissy toward Rosie.

T.C., as nosy as he was, had somehow been unaware of Leeza being somewhat of a friend to Rosie. But right now, no one was paying any attention to Leeza. While all the fuss was going on, the lovely Angora, suffering from her own problems, vanished from the barn.

Where had she gone?

Chapter 9.

THE BULL WHIP

Word had meandered through the carnival concerning Rossi's inhumane treatment of the burro. Several of the ride operators had seen it happen, but so far no one had done anything about it.

Then Kirk Locks, who operated the Ferris wheel, caught Rossi hitting Piston over the head with that cussed bull whip. Angered by the abuse, Kirk grabbed the whip and slowly backed away a few feet, never taking his eyes off Rossi. With a firm, determined grip on the wooden handle, he cracked the whip to the right side of Rossi's head and then to the left. Kirk was obviously an expert in its' use.

Victor Rossi stood perfectly still. He had watched Kirk handle a bull whip before. He knew the man was capable of slicing both his ears from his head, one after the other. Actually, this young man was so good with the bull whip, he could peel an orange and never spill a bit of juice.

"You stole my whip, old man!" Kirk shoved the leather under Rossi's nose. "See here! My initials! Right where Billy Fairchild burned them in when he made this whip for me. If Billy had caught you causing hurt to an animal with this whip that he made with his own hands, God help you, man! The eyes from your head would be looking up at you from the ground." Kirk gathered the braided leather around his arm. He walked a few feet away, then turned and shook his finger at Rossi. "I'm passing the word about you. Wouldn't mind coming back here and doing to you what I saw you doing to that animal."

Piston hoped that Kirk would go a little further. Let Rossi have it with that whip! Call the cops! Do anything but walk away!

Victor Rossi silently mouthed insults and cuss words at the man's back. Had those words fallen upon Kirk's ears, Rossi would have lost both of his.

Carnival people have always had the reputation of helping each other, like one big family. Animals should be included in that family, one would think.

The midget had a good heart and wanted to help Piston, but he was rightfully afraid of Rossi. John Patton gave help when it was badly needed, once, and then left the state. Kirk Lock had come to the aid of the burro, but was he truly concerned about Piston,

or was he primarily retrieving his bull whip? Piston
wondered. A man like Rossi required constant watching. Piston was stolen property! Didn't anybody no-
tice, or care? Surely other people were around when
the burro was forced to pack such heavy loads that he
nearly pulled his insides out. Wouldn't you think
someone would call the authorities? Rossi had no
right to any animal, not the way he treated one.

The carnival people were all extremely busy. Each
worker and performer lived in a fast moving world of
his own. Many times someone would come close to
catching Rossi when he whaled away on the poor
beast. But he was definitely a clever, devious man, always on the lookout, not wanting to be found out.
He kept to himself. For that matter, no one trusted
him or could stand to be near him.

All this while Piston had stayed tied to a humon-
gous pile of canvas and rope. With Kirk out of the
way, Victor yelled at his unhappy, ill-gotten, overworked servant. Quickly, he glanced around, and seeing no one looking in his direction, he jerked at the
animal's halter. Piston made little progress with the
load. A caring man would have divided the weight
and made two trips.

The tents were coming down. Trucks were again
being loaded. There would be no rest. Tomorrow the
Vagabond Carnival Company would leave Seattle and
head for Portland, Oregon. Piston overheard carnival

people talking about the summer and fall schedule. After Portland, they would move south to Salem, for the Oregon State Fair. The big one, eleven days. Piston knew that Salem was close to his old home at Glenn and Alice Greystone's. How nice it would be to be there again with Stinger and those who cared about him.

Kirk Locks, the midget, and a couple of other carnival people dropped by Rossi's truck to make absolutely sure that Piston was not chained for the trip to Portland.

"Leave us alone!" Rossi shouted, as the men looked on. "He's my mule, not yours!"

"He's not a mule," the midget spoke more bravely, not being alone with Rossi, "he's a small burro!"

"Oh, yeah, you know so much! Your brain is as weak as your body. Mind your own business!" Rossi closed the back door to his rig and hurried to get into the cab.

The men agreed to stay close to Rossi's truck and keep an eye on him. The midget was grateful that someone besides he had taken an interest in the burro. He had named Piston "Little Grey".

This time, the moving trip was more pleasant. Every time Rossi looked over his shoulder or in his rear view mirror, sure enough, he was being watched. Now and then, he faked an act of kindness to the animal. This time he had placed an armload of straw bedding in the truck for Piston. Piston could not believe his good fortune.

How he would love to stand up to Rossi! He passed the dreary miles dreaming, about just how he could do it.

"How about right now," he thought. Oh, how he wanted to stand up, kick that stinking, lousy truck apart and run like the wind. But he knew he couldn't. Each day he grew more tired and thin than the day before. The very best he could hope for today would be to rest on the straw. That would be nice.

There would be more heavy loads to lift and pull when they reached Portland. Perhaps if he were more rested and could manage heavier loads, maybe then Rossi would not beat him so much. Maybe he'd even get more to eat. All this was going on in the sad little fellow's head. Had he given up?

The trucks in the caravan had pulled into a rest area. From what Piston could hear, it sounded like the radiator on Rossi's truck was spewing hot steam. Rossi opened up the back door to grab a bucket. While he was gone to get water, the midget showed up with kind works for Piston.

"Are you resting, Little Grey?" he asked. "I'll make sure you get a bite to eat at lunch time." The midget had the best of intentions. But when lunch time arrived, he couldn't get close enough to the truck to keep his word. Rossi had parked under a

The trucks in the caravan pulled into a rest area.

large tree. He did not get far from his truck. From the cab of his truck, he fetched a thermos of something, and some bananas. There was a green lawn chair tied to the side of his truck. He opened it up, placing it, where do you suppose? At the back door of his truck, defying anyone to come near.

It was hot in the truck. The carrier was a solid wooden box with only two small windows, one on the left and one on the right. They were quite a distance from the floor. Piston could not see out and no one could see in.

"I deserve this life," the burro told himself. "I did nothing but cause trouble when the Greystones had me. All I ever wanted to do was get out of the pasture and see what the rest of the world looked like. Now look at me! I travel all the time. But all I ever get to see is the inside of a smelly truck and the grotesque, hard-featured face of one Victor Rossi.

"Maybe it was because Stinger and I had the full Nevada range to ramble around in before we were adopted; maybe that's why the pasture was not enough room for me. It did seem small. And those fences! Wow! How does anyone stand fences? But we had it good there, Stinger and I. Why wasn't I satisfied? What's my problem?" Piston asked himself. "We had delectable green grass, a fresh stream to drink from, no work, grain in the barn every morning and the best smelling alfalfa in the world anytime we wanted it. The Greystones were wonderful to us. They wanted us. They wanted nothing more than to give two burros a home.

"Scrud! If I just had one more chance! I'd be a real angel! I'd stay home. I'd eat and sleep and be happy. If a storm came up and there was thunder and lightning, I'd lie down and go to sleep. I wouldn't get scared and kick barns apart and hurt poor old hogs, ever again. But what if ---, what if I couldn't help myself? Storms make me crazy!"

Piston thought and thought before he dropped off to sleep, tired, hungry and thirsty. But there was not a thing he could do about it.

Perchance in Portland things would be better.

"I will get away soon, somehow," he told himself. "I must not give up."

Chapter 10.

WHERE IS LEEZA

Though Little Prissy thought nothing of it, she was the only one of the sows who could carry on a conversation with a human. She had picked it up from Priscilla, her mother. Mama was the only human she could communicate with.

"All you have to do is take the time to listen," Mama explained to Papa. But he had no intention of spending his time in such a fashion. He thought it was a little silly. Though he knew full well that Mama and Prissy understood each other, sometimes it provoked him to think Mama could and he couldn't.

Today the animals waited for Mama's arrival. Prissy had a question to ask her. It was a matter of urgency!

At 7:00 o'clock, Papa did the morning feeding, alone. It was 9:30 a.m. when Mama finally came in to bottle-feed Mabel's orphan pigs. Bottle feeding had been cut down to twice daily, now that the pigs were eating solid pellets and doing extremely well. Prissy was still next door to the litter.

"Mama, can you hear me?" Prissy asked above the squealing pigs who were waiting impatiently for their turn.

Mama laughed at her. "Not very well," she answered, watching the happy little white Landrace in her arms. While he tugged at the nipple, she noticed for the umpteenth time how much he resembled Mabel. "I'll be over there in a few minutes, darling," she told Prissy.

The Tom Cat was in Little Prissy's pen. He wanted to be there when the question was answered.

All sixteen of Prissy's pigs were in the corner creep of the pen, sleeping peacefully. They were piled up on each other, like cordwood. First, Mama took a look at them before turning her attenion to their mother.

"We have a problem, Mama," Little Prissy began. "T.C. is pretty worried and so am I. Something has happened to Leeza! We haven't seen her for two days. She hasn't been in here, and Tom Cat has looked all over the farm for her. Have you seen her? Is she in the house?" Prissy asked. Tom Cat looked on anxiously.

Mama could see how concerned they were.

"I'm sorry, my friends, I wish I had a better answer for you, but I haven't seen her either. She isn't in the house. She may have been down around the house, though. Several cats eat food from the back porch at night. Some of them are pretty wild. They come down from the timber. Papa and I never see them. We just put out the food and it always disappears."

Prissy was busy repeating everything to T.C.

Mama picked up the cat. "That lovely Leeza has you pretty worried, doesn't she? You worried us too, Tom Cat, when you were gone for so long. But don't worry, she will be back. How could she possibly walk away from a handsome fellow like you?" Mama smiled.

"Do you think she's in trouble?" Prissy asked. "Maybe tangled up in some vine or blackberry thicket?"

"I hope not, darling. I'll tell Papa. We'll take a good look around for her."

She didn't have to wait long to keep her word. Papa drove up in front of the barn on the tractor. It was loud.

"Did you have a look at Rosie?" Papa asked.

"No, not yet. Should I?" Mama questioned, figuring he had already done it.

"Today is her big day. Says so on the calendar, anyway," Papa grinned.

"Papa, have you seen Leeza around anywhere?" she asked. Prissy and T.C. listened.

"Leeza? No! Isn't she with T.C.?" he asked. Papa was used to seeing them together.

"No. Prissy says they haven't seen her for two whole days."

"You been talkin' to that hog again?" Papa laughed.

"Yes, I have," she answered. "I think we ought to have a look around, don't you?"

"O.K., but let me have a look at Rosie first," Papa spent a few minutes in Rosie's pen. She was on her feet eating. A hog seldom eats anything just before her litter is born. The extra bedding was still in the corner. When it's near the time for her pigs to be born, she will make a fresh bed with her straw. Then she will lie down, rest and wait. Rosie was not yet ready to have pigs.

Off went Mama, Papa and T.C., looking for Leeza. They made a thorough search, but there were many buildings and great places to hide. If Leeza did not want to be found, they would not be able to find her.

Early that morning, Papa had seen Maggie chasing a fox back to the timber. Maggie kept the varmints away from the chicken house. Although Papa had never heard of foxes bothering the cats, he wondered about it just the same.

Going back to the farrowing barn with no good news did not give Mama any pleasure, but it had to be done.

"I'm sorry, my friends, but we were unable to find Leeza," Mama reported sorrowfully. "We will keep looking. I'll watch carefully this evening as soon as I hear a cat on the back porch at the feed. She might come."

"Tell us if she does, so we know she's all right," Prissy requested. The little sow was truly concerned. "Why would she stay away, Mama? Doesn't she know we are worried about her? Doesn't she know we care?"

"That's a good question, Prissy. Papa and I care about her too. We'll keep looking."

The disappearance of the cat was thoroughly discussed at the supper table.

"I think she's about ready to have kittens," Papa guessed. "I've been dishing out extra goat's milk for her down at the barn. She licks up every drop."

"I'll bet she's had those kittens. But why is she hiding?" Mama asked.

"Who knows! I'll bet a dollar she's all right. She will come walking out of one of the buildings in a few days with a kitten in her mouth. Papa laughed. "Now tell me about tomorrow. Are we going to the State Fair?" Papa inquired.

"I wouldn't miss it," Mama sounded happy to be

getting a day off.

"Well, it depends on Rosie whether I get to go or not. Knowing that cranky sow, she'll want to have her pigs about the time I want to leave for the fair."

Mama would go for sure, with their daughter, Deana. Papa didn't care. He liked to see them go and have a good time. He'd make it eventually.

"I know you want to go to see all the livestock," Mama told him. "I promised the grandkids that I would take them all, on Thursday."

"That's day after tomorrow," he said.

"Right! I hope I'm ready for all those kids," she laughed. "I've doubled up on my vitamins!"

"I'll go with you for sure on Thursday. You'll need some help!" he said.

Sometime in the evening, long after dark, Mama heard cats on the back porch. Quickly she hurried to the door to have a look.

The cats were frightened and ran. It was awfully dark. But she was almost positive she recognized one of them.

Chapter 11.

NO KIDS OR PIGS

When the sun came up the next morning, Mama was sure it was the most beautiful day she had ever seen. A great day for the fair!

But first, before she could think about that, there were a few things she must attend to here at home.

Papa had been to the farrowing barn and reported that Rosie was off her feed and was making her nest. Pigs would be arriving in a couple of hours. Just as Papa predicted, he would have to stay at home. Mama would go on to the fair with Deana.

First, she cleared the kitchen table and then made the beds. She was eager to get outside, for she was certain it was Leeza she had seen last night, running in the direction of the old machine shed. But, it had been quite dark.

Mama loved the old machine shed. It was there that a special pen had been built for Priscilla when

Leeza hissed and growled at Mama.

she outgrew the house. Priscilla had been a runt, lain on by her mother and badly hurt. Mama and Papa took her in and made her well. She lived in the house, could turn the television on and off with her nose; she could answer the telephone and do so many other things. There were fond memories of her here, in the machine shed.

The search for Leeza turned out to be a short one. First one kitten's meow was heard and then another. Following the sound, Mama walked toward the old barrel in the corner. There they were, Leeza and four kittens, behind the barrel on an old feed sack.

The new mother was not happy at being found. She hissed and growled. Mama left immediately.

"What's the matter with her?" Mama asked herself, puzzled by the cat's reaction, and slightly disappointed. "Leeza should know by now that we love all of our animals. We wouldn't hurt her babies." Mama went straight to the farrowing barn to report her findings.

During the next few minutes, Leeza moved her kittens up the ladder to a new spot in the hay loft. Even though she chose to keep hidden, the family was doing fine.

Mama picked up her daughter in Salem and headed for the fair. Deana was glad to get away from the kids for a day. She had four, all eager to be taken to the fair tomorrow by their grandparents. It was an annual event, a family tradition.

Today was a day of leisure for Mama and Deana. The two of them seldom had a day to be together without having to tend kids or pigs.

The commercial buildings were alive with vendors and buyers. At each bend in the aisle another huckster delivered his well-rehearsed pitch. Each one had a little microphone around his neck and spoke to various sized crowds. Lookers and buyers came and went.

Opportunities to buy household gadgets were plentiful. No-stick skillets, many brands. To make a point, one fellow kept burning cheese in a little coated frying pan. He wiped it out with a paper towel to show that the skillet was not harmed.

Deana looked at her mother. "Mom, have you ever burned cheese in a skillet?"

"No, I never have!" Mama answered.

"Me neither!" she laughed. "I guess we don't need one of these."

The hucksters were not short of business. It seemed to be profitable to the fellow burning up all that cheese. He was doing his cheese trick with one hand while making change with the other.

Mama and Deana looked at slicers, dicers, shakers, cookie makers and a sharp knife that could cut a tomato without losing juice. The knife salesman was a blonde, blue-eyed, fast-talking fellow. Every few moments, he would drag the blade of the knife across a piece of steel pipe. The knife remained sharp. Quite a tool indeed. Both Mama and Deana decided they must have one. Later, Deana returned to buy a second one for her neighbor, Ruth, who was at home keeping an eye on all the kids.

After the commercial buildings had been thoroughly examined, they headed for the arts and crafts area, and then it was time for a cold lemonade. The day passed quickly. At two p.m. they sat down to rest and enjoy a show by the Oak Ridge Boys. Tomorrow Roy Clark would be there.

"I hope he plays the 'Orange Blossom Special',"

Mama smiled. "Remember how Priscilla loved Roy Clark's banjo music?"

Deana looked at her mother. "You still think about her, don't you, Mom?"

"Something is always happening to remind me of her. She was so funny."

For a few minutes they watched some Duroc sows being judged.

"Matt Ferrell was right, Deana. Papa would have walked away with all the blue ribbons. I haven't seen anything here as good looking as our own hogs." Mama wished Papa was there. "But he will see it all later," she thought.

Before long they would have to head for home. Deana came up with a brainstorm.

"Let's go back to the carnival area. You can see what you'll be getting into tomorrow."

"That's a great idea," Mama answered.

Loud music permeated the entire area. You could hear it long before you got to the site. It hit Mama's ear drums with a blast sufficient to blow out a truck tire. She placed her hands over her ears.

"Tomorrow, I'm wearing ear plugs," she announced. "How do the kids stand this stuff?"

A young man with a strange hair cut and an earring in his nose, ran into Mama. She gave him a dirty look.

The carnival area was large. They stood in the

midst of the Vagabond Carnival Company. There were dozens of bright colored rides, all kinds, loaded with screaming, yelling youngsters, having a good time. The lines to the rides were long. The area was enclosed by a tall wire fence, with numerous gates and turnstiles for convenient coming and going.

Behind the fence, trucks and trailers were parked, belonging to the carnival and to people who traveled with the carnival.

Mama read the admissions sign on the ticket office to get an idea of how much it was going to cost her to bring all the kids. She nearly fainted. The price per ride was high; it would cost a mint of money. But she was not about to disappoint the kids. She had made them a promise and that promise would be kept.

Then something wonderful happened. A little family stood nearby. They were discussing the price of the rides. They were trying to figure out how they could get the most for their money.

Deana overheard the young lady in the ticket booth tell the family that tomorrow all the rides would be free from 10 a.m to 2 p.m., sponsored by the local merchants.

"Mom, you're in luck!" Deana laughed.

"How about that! We picked the best day to come and didn't even know it."

The Ferris wheel was in back of the ticket booth,

and beyond the metal fence something caught Mama's eye. There stood a poor, dirty little burro, tied to a truck. It was sad and lonely looking. She felt sorry for the animal. "It's about the same size as Piston," she thought, wondering whatever happened to him. Mama had no idea she was looking at Piston. How could she know? There was no resemblance. None whatsoever. The Piston she knew was healthy, clean and full bodied. He was never sad and had no appearance of being so. The Piston she knew was clever, good natured and ornery. He would never put up with being tied to a truck.

If Mama had only known the truth, things would have changed for the better for Piston. For today at least, the burro's luck was still running bad.

Chapter 12.

THE MORNING OF THE FAIR

The phone rang. Deana was calling at the insistance of the kids.

"How soon are you going to be here, Mom, and can they take one more kid? This kid has her own money." It was only seven a.m. The fair grounds wouldn't open for three more hours.

"I'll be there at 9:30," Mama answered. "And yes, they can take another kid. Be sure every one of them is wearing a watch, like we planned." If you went with Mama you had to wear a watch. When she got them to the fair, she would tell them why!

"Mom, they want you to make it nine instead of 9:30. There will be a crowd," Deana passed on the message from the kids.

"I'll try! Papa will come in later in the pickup. He's got some running around to do. But he promised me he'd be there by noon to give me a hand."

Mama wasn't telling Deana everything. No use to
worry the kids. There was a small crises at the barn.
The vet was there, with Papa. Two of Rosie's four-
teen pigs were born with pockets of fluid under their
hide. The doctor hoped he could remove all the ex-
cess with a needle.

Christina and Sara were extremely fond of all the
pigs. Mama didn't want them to worry. No kid should
have to worry about anything on fair day.

After the phone call, Mama headed for the chick-
en house to see if any more eggs had hatched. Scram-
led Eggs and her chicks were scratching in the back
yard. Four hens were in nesting boxes. Almost all the
eggs had hatched. Newborns peeked out from under
their mothers. Mama gathered all the empty shells
and threw them away.

By the time Mama got to the barn, the vet had
gone.

"Rosie's babies didn't care much for the needle,"
Papa said.

"I don't blame them. They look better," Mama
noticed, picking up one in each hand. But the pigs
had been handled enough. They began to squeal.
Down they went.

"So, all right, I won't hold you. I just wanted to
tell you how much better you look," she told the
pigs.

"Your babies are lovely, Rosie, just like you. And

Scrambled Eggs and her chicks.

they are all going to be just fine, you'll see." Mama
said to Rosie, hoping that she understood.

Tom Cat came in to Rosie's pen and began to
nose around. Little Prissy had asked him to be nice to
Rosie. He would try, but he wouldn't promise anything. Prissy had told him about a little sign that hung
on the wall above Papa's desk in the house. Priscilla
had told her about it. It read, "Love Your Enemies. It
Drives Them Nuts."

T.C. had thought about that a lot. "Maybe that's
what the Porker is doing to Rosie, being nice to her

and driving her nuts." T.C. liked that idea very much. He would give it a try and see what loving misery he could concoct for Rosie.

Prissy's sixteen babies were a handful for their mother. She told Mama they were the peskiest litter ever, but she loved them, every one.

"Did you know Leeza moved her kittens again?" Little Prissy asked Mama.

"How do you know that, Prissy?" Mama asked.

"When you told me they were in the machine shed, T.C. went looking for her. When he got there, he saw her moving the fourth kitten up the ladder to the hay loft. She doesn't want you around her babies, Mama."

Mama was surprised and a little hurt. "Why, darling? I thought she liked me."

"She does! But she's afraid you'll take her kittens away from her and sell them." Prissy told her.

"What? Where did she get an idea like that?"

"Who knows? Remember how miserable I was when I thought you were going to sell me?" Prissy asked. Mama nodded. "I know how she must be feeling. The Killians always sold her babies for a lot of money."

Little Prissy explained that Tom Cat had finally gotten Leeza to tell him why she hid her kittens.

"Well, Papa and I aren't the Killians, and we would never sell her kittens."

Mama headed for the house to get ready for the fair.

Then Mama laughed. "Leeza may be a purebred Angora, but her kittens, ---well, Prissy, they are half barn tabby cat, just like that handsome devil of a Tom Cat."

"I see what you mean," Prissy grinned. "I'll tell T.C. to let Leeza know that her kittens are hers to keep."

Mama headed for the house to get ready for the fair. She had no way of knowing that today at the fair, events would happen that her family would talk about for the rest of their lives.

Chapter 13.

THE STATE FAIR

Victor Rossi was in a foul mood. Last night, he had spotted a truck making a delivery to the lunch counter in the stadium where the horse races are held. Rossi watched and waited. The driver loaded up a hand truck with cases of beer and disappeared into the building. In a matter of seconds, Rossi had stolen a case of beer from the truck, whipped it into the gunny sack attached to Piston's harness, and off they went.

As usual, he chained the burro to the back of the truck. He retired to his trailer and commenced swigging down the beer. Rossi could not handle drinking. In less than an hour he was crowing like a rooster, crashing into things. He was loud and crazy. He picked up a chair and slammed it down on the table. The little chair broke into a dozen pieces. He kept on drinking.

Piston was worried. "What if he comes out of his trailer? Will I get beat up again?" he asked himself. A single tear trailed down the little fellow's face. He was used to being tired and hungry, but he had never gotten used to being tied in one spot. The entire area around Rossi's place smelled terrible, and the warm sun made it even worse. Misery was Piston's companion, day in and day out.

There were no more favors of food and fresh water from the midget. He was a frail little man, terrified by Rossi. Now more than ever. The last time he brought food, Rossi caught him, flew into a rage, followed the frightened man home and ripped apart the inside of his trailer. After that, the midget was too afraid to come around.

But today was the morning after all that drinking. The wicked old man was sick. Last night he crowed like a rooster; this morning he groaned like an injured ape.

Piston looked on with a satisfied interest as Rossi suffered. Rossi had made fun of the midget's appearance. Today Rossi's eyes were blood-red and his skin a sickly green. Worst of all, his breath smelled as if he'd had a burnt skunk-and-onion breakfast.

Rossi was getting paid back for drinking and stealing.

During all this hullabaloo, the burro had enjoyed

a few extremely happy, entertaining moments. It all happened last night when Rossi fell down the steps of his trailer, landing squarely on his back, face up to the stars. He was out cold in a drunken stupor.

Piston loved it! He laughed and brayed and laughed some more.

"Are we having fun yet?" Piston shouted at Rossi. He really made the most of the moment and laughed while he could.

Mama and seven kids had been in the carnival area since the gates opened at 10 o'clock. Before she picked up their passes, she had gathered them around her to synchronize their watches. When you went with Mama you reported in every two hours. Now it was exactly noon. She counted the seven heads around her and pointed toward the food alley. It was difficult to talk over the loud music. But she got no takers on food. No one was ready to eat except Shawn, and for once in his life he was willing to give up food, temporarily, if they could ride more rides.

"There are two more hours to ride free, Grandma," Christina reported hurriedly. It was obvious she was anxious to get back to the rides.

"Yeah, Gram, look at all the money you're saving," Sara laughed. Mama had to agree with Sara. She waved at them as if she were shooing flies, "Go on! Have fun! Meet me right here at two o'clock."

Christina had brought along her friend, Danita.

Sara had invited Jenny, a neighbor and best friend since they were three years old. Karen Morey came with Shawn. These two were only a week apart in their ages and enjoyed riding the same rides. Steven was only five. He stayed with his grandmother and rode the kiddie rides. Now and then he was taken along on a "big kid" ride.

Once, he and Mama rode the Ferris wheel. When they were moving slowly upward, while the seats were being emptied and refilled, Mama happened to look down for a moment. On the other side of the fence stood that same thin, little burro that she had seen the day before.

"Why would anyone tie an animal on such a short rope? And why is he so thin?" Mama asked herself. *"He's not tied with a rope, but with a rusty, heavy chain,"* she observed. *That was uncalled for!* Mama pointed out the burro to Steven.

"See, Steven, there's a poor little burro down there. Doesn't he look sad?"

Steven looked down at him. As the Ferris wheel went around and around, up and down, he never took his eyes off the burro.

"Can we take him something to eat?" Steven asked-ed.

"We don't have anything to take him, honey. But you're right about wanting to feed him. He looks like he could use some good meals." Mama wished there was something they could do to help him.

At 2:00 o'clock a tired, happy bunch of kids converged on food alley. Mama and Steven had scouted out the best place. If anybody knew what this pack of kids liked to eat, Mama did. She loved to feed them whatever they liked to eat.

It would be great fair food, giant hamburgers, curly fries, corn on the cob and lemonade.

Mama had left a message at the ticket office for Papa. Two o'clock found him lining up with everybody else, ordering food. Rows of picnic tables were set up end-to-end under a broad red and white striped canvas canopy.

There was no holding back; everybody porked down food with a most energetic motion. Their appetites matched the food; their thirst, the large paper cups of lemonade.

Shawn was never without his powerful craving for food. His friend Karen was a magician when it came to curly fries: She made them quickly disappear.

Each of them gave a report. Christina and Danita had ridden the Enterprise eight times and the Scrambler, nine. Sara perferred the Octopus, Jenny the Tobogan. Shawn and Karen like Gravitation. Steven liked riding the little roller coaster and the big Ferris wheel with grandma.

"We saw a sad little grey donkey," Steven told his grandfather. "Didn't we, Grandma?"

"Yes we did, Steven," Mama answered. Steven had thought of little else. He was still thinking about it when the party broke up into pairs and headed in different directions, but not before Mama and Papa had given out orders where and when to meet together again. Once again they synchronized their watches. All but Karen; she had lost hers somewhere, probably on a ride. She promised she would look at Shawn's watch when she wanted to know the time. It was 2:55 p.m. At 6 o'clock they would meet again to feed anybody who was hungry. Shawn would be hungry; Shawn was always hungry.

Steven would stay with Mama and Papa until seven o'clock. The Roy Clark show would begin at eight, and Mama felt she and Papa must be there by seven to get a good seat.

At that time, Steven would go with the big kids, who promised to stay together after seven. They promised to trade off tending him, so he could ride some rides too. But for now, Steven wanted to go with Mama and Papa to get his picture taken with a chimpanzee.

When he got near the chimp, he almost changed his mind. But after he watched a boy smaller than he with the chimp, he decided he was brave enough to go through with it.

He sat still when the man placed the chimp on his lap. On cue, the animal put his arm around Steven's neck and smiled toward the camera. It was a cute photo.

"This animal doesn't look sad and hungry," Steven thought. He was reminded again of the poor little burro, and wondered if there was something he could do to help.

"There ought to be a way," Steven thought.

What was Steven planning?

Chapter 14.

STEVEN GETS LOST

The ampitheater where the Roy Clark show was presented was some distance from the carnival rides. Good thing! Otherwise, the loud music from the rides would drown out all the entertainment.

Steven felt like a big person now that he was with the older kids. He pulled a dollar out of his pocket and announced that he was getting a corn-on-the-cob.

"Give me a big one," he told the lady in the yellow dress. "No butter." Now, he stood there with the ear of corn in one hand and a napkin in the other.

Since the kids had promised Mama they would stay together, they would have to wait until Steven ate his corn. No food was allowed on the rides. It wasn't too big a decision. They just looked for a long line and got in it.

Steven waited until no one was paying any

Steven felt like a big person now.

attention to him and then he slipped away. In seconds he was out of sight. The evening crowd was shoulder to shoulder.

Christina reached down to put her hand on Steven. He wasn't there. It was sudden fear. She began calling for him, louder and louder. Tears welled up in her eyes.

"Mom will kill us," Sara cried. "One of us should have held his hand."

"How? I had him by the hand until he bought that darned ear of corn," Christina told her. "He's somewhere with an ear of corn in one hand and a napkin in the other. We'll search in pairs for five minutes and then return here. Everybody be careful. Stay with your partner. If we don't find him in three, five-minute tries, we'll tell the security people."

Shawn and Karen were the youngest, only ten. Christina took Shawn with her and Danita took Karen. Sara and Jenny would search together. They started off in different directions. They were six worried youngsters.

At the end of five minutes no one had been successful. In ten minutes, still no sign of Steven, nor in fifteen.

Their fear increased. Where was he? They had searched all the rides, and all around the rides, had asked people if they'd seen him. But it was difficult. There were lots of five year old boys who fit his description, and a few of them were eating corn on the cob.

Steven was a bright, thoughtful little guy. It wasn't like him to wander off like that and worry people.

Christina, as the oldest, was trying her best to be calm and organized. Being organized was her best trait. But this was nerveracking. These things happened to other people, not to her. She felt sick.

"Guys, we've got to tell our grandparents," she told them.

"Not me!" Shawn was scared they'd be in big trouble. "I'm not tellin' them!"

Sara and Jenny offered to do it. "They've got to know, Shawn. I don't think we'll have too much trouble finding them. They're down close to the front. " Off they ran.

Security tried to help. But there were several lost children. There were also a few drunks and crazies out there giving them trouble. One comforting thought was, that no child had ever been abducted from this fair grounds. One of the men had told them. But the kids were so upset they began to imagine the worst.

Sara and Jenny returned with Mama and Papa.

Christina began to cry. "I'm so sorry he got away from us! But his hands were full and I didn't have a hand to grab hold of."

"It's nobody's fault, Christina. We'll find him.

He's a curious five year old boy!" Mama tried to comfort her granddaughter, trying all the while to hide her own fears.

Papa talked with a young security woman who had been staying there with the kids. She briefed him on what was being done to find his grandson.

Mama tried to think back over the day with Steven. What did he like best? Where would he go? She said a silent prayer.

"Help us, Heavenly Father, please help us find our Steven, he's only five. You know how much he means to us."

Then Mama had a thought, as if her prayer had been answered.

"Christina, did you say he had an ear of corn in his hand?" she asked. Christina nodded.

"I don't think he'd even taken a bite of it," Jenny remembered.

Mama's face changed. She was half smiling. "Papa, stay here with the kids. Christina and Sara, come with me." Mama had an idea, she sounded determined about something, but nobody knew what, except her.

She took the girls by the hands. "Come on!" she said. "I don't know how you kids stand this loud music!" They headed in the direction of the Ferris wheel. The lights were so bright on the rides, it was like daytime. Mama led the way, pulling the girls

"Do you want your hands stamped?"

through the crowd. Around the Ferris wheel they went, heading for an exit gate in the fence.

"Are we leaving?" Sara looked surprised. "Are you that mad at us?"

"We're not leaving," Mama answered as she pulled the girls through the turnstile.

"Do you want your hands stamped?" Asked the tired looking fellow at the gate.

"What?" Mama asked, her mind was on something

else.

"Will you be returning?" he asked.

"Yes! Stamp us!" she said quickly. He did, with a green Oregon pine tree.

The girls exchanged glances. Had Mama gone nuts? Outside the gate, she pulled them past a couple of little house trailers. Then they passed a truck, Victor Rossi's truck.

And there Steven was, at the rear of the truck. He had his arms wrapped tightly around the neck of the dirty, little grey burro he had seen from the Ferris wheel. His knees were soiled where he had knelt on the filthy ground. Also on the ground lay the corn cob. It was obvious; Steven had brought some feed to the sad little animal.

"Darling, we were so worried about you," Christina cried.

"I just wanted to feed the hungry burro," Steven told them. "He's so nice. I didn't mean to worry you."

"Let's go find everybody, Steven. They'll want to know that you're safe. We thought you were lost." Sara led Steven back through the turnstile. Mama followed. Christina kept looking at the burro. She wondered if all burros look alike.

What a relief when all nine of them were back together again.

Mama and Papa thanked Security and headed

back to the ampitheater. Some one was saving their seats. This time they took Steven with them.

When they were out of sight, Christina took Sara aside.

"Sara, I could be wrong, but I believe that burro is Piston."

"Piston?" Sara looked surprised.

The girls looked at each other. "Let's check it out, Sara," Christina said, with a twinkle in her eye.

"Yes! Let's."

Chapter 15.

IS IT PISTON

"**D**o you really think *that* burro is Piston, Christy? Don't you think Grandma would have recognized him?" Sara asked.

"Think about it, Sara. Grandma was more concerned about Steven than she was letting on. That's why she didn't pay any attention to the burro. If it hadn't been for Steven, I feel sure she would have recognized him, immediately," Christina said.

Danita, Jenny, Shawn and Karen listened as Christina and Sara told them what they intended to do.

"Will you guys come with us?" Sara asked.

Danita and Jenny thought it sounded like a great adventure. Karen was afraid they might get into trouble. Shawn wanted to go get some more curly fries.

"Shawn, you've already had two helpings since lunch," Jenny reminded him. But did Shawn care?

97

"What's an extra little curly fry or two among friends?" he giggled.

"Be serious, Shawn. Let's go check out this burro." Christina told him. She headed for the gate. The rest followed.

Christina and Sara had seen Piston several times at the Greystones. Once, when he had gotten out and come to visit the hogs, the girls helped Papa take him home. Of course he looked different then. In his present condition, how could the girls be sure? But there was something about this burro that caught Christina's eye. What was it?

One by one they exited through the turnstile. Those who hadn't done so already, got their hands stamped with an Oregon pine tree. Shawn kept looking at his, not paying any attention to where he was going. He came to a sudden stop! He had run into a large handbag that was hanging from a fat lady's arm.

Karen giggled as Shawn turned to the "handbag" and said politely, "Well, ---excuse ---me!"

Piston still stood in the same spot, looking just as forlorn as he had when Steven and Mama saw him earlier in the day. Once again, he had found a friend, but the friend had vanished, just like the others.

Christina and Sara began calling him by name.

"Piston! Piston! Is that you?"

Piston looked up as if awakening from a deep sleep. His eyes sparkled with joy. He turned his chin to the heavens and let out the happiest bray of his life. Here were humans he recognized from a better time he had known, and who seemed to recognize him.

"Can they help me?" Piston asked himself. His braying continued loud enough to attract the attention of one Victor Rossi.

Rossi poked his angry face out the door of the trailer to investigate. How dare "his" beast make a sound? When he saw the kids with Piston, he flew into a rage. He screamed vulgar, vile words. He waved his arms and headed in the direction of the kids, frightening them.

The kids took off, but they ran no farther than the turnstile. Christina and Sara did not scare easily.

Poor Karen was terrified.

"Let's get out of here," she cried.

The fellow at the turnstile saw what happened. He was concerned for their safety.

"Hey, kids, better stay away from that burro. That old codger who owns him is plenty ornery and from what I've heard tonight, he's about half drunk already."

Reluctantly, all six of them went back through the turnstile. Well, all but Karen; she was not a bit reluctant. She didn't want any part of that burro or the scary, gross, old man, as she called him.

The girls hadn't given up, not those girls. They

just had to decide on their next move. More determined than ever, they crept along the inside of the fence until they were directly behind Rossi's trailer. They could hear Rossi's voice above the din of the carnival. He was back inside the trailer now, swilling down more of the beer he had stolen the night before.

"Now what do we do?" Danita asked.

"That *was* Piston, Christy!" Sara said anxiously. "How did you ever recognize him? Poor thing! He looks awful!"

"He looks like he's about ready to die. Something's really wrong here," Christina said.

A young man at the Ferris wheel was keeping an eye on the youngsters. It was Kirk Locks. From his work station, he could see everything that went on around Rossi's truck and trailer. This was the fellow who had taken his bull whip away from Rossi and threatened to use it on him if he saw the burro being mistreated again. But, Kirk didn't always see everything. Many times, Piston had wished for Kirk.

Kirk left his associates in charge of the running of the ride so he could have a word with this group of kids.

"Did Rossi hurt any of you?" he asked as he came toward them.

They looked at each other, feeling safe since there were six of them.

"Who is Rossi?" Karen asked.

"The loud mouth drunk who lives in that trailer over there," he said, pointing in that direction.

"Why did you think he might hurt us?" Christina asked.

"Because he's a brutal, cold-hearted hound. Not fit to be called a human. God knows he's hurt that poor animal of his enough times. You'd better stay away from there. There's no telling what he'll do to you kids if you mess around the animal."

"How long has he had the burro?" Jenny asked. Christina was about to ask the same question.

"Just got him this summer some place. He worked his last one to death! All of us try to keep an eye on him, hoping we can prevent his cruelty to the animal. Problem is, we can't watch him all the time," Kirk told them. "Why are you kids so interested in that burro? Oh, by the way, my name is Kirk Locks. I run the Ferris wheel."

Kirk had given them a lot of information. He seemed to be a man who could be trusted, but the youngsters were not ready to reveal their venture to anyone just yet.

"Uh, well, we like animals," Sara sputtered.

"Especially burros," Danita added.

Kirk had to return to his job. "Take my advice, kids; don't go back there anymore."

No sooner had he left than a very strange thing

happened. They had never met a midget. But coming toward them was a small, pale, miniature man. He stopped a few feet from them, by the fence. He was staring at Piston. The kids were staring at him. It was a stand off.

What a strange person, this little midget. He was truly afraid of Rossi but still very concerned about the burro.

Shawn walked nearer the man. He looked at Shawn. "I call the burro, 'Little Grey'."

"Why?" Shawn asked. "Is that what the man in the trailer calls him?" Shawn had not called Rossi the owner, but rather, the man in the trailer.

"No!" He studied the face of each youngster. "Do you know something about 'Little Grey'?" he asked.

No one answered, arousing suspicion. Again they heard Rossi's raving, above the sound of the carnival.

"Do you work for the carnival?" Christina asked him.

The man nodded.

"Was the carnival in Boise, Idaho this summer?" Christina continued.

"No, not Boise."

Sara and Christina exchanged looks. The carnival would have to have been in Boise, or at least Rossi would have had to be in Boise, if he was the thief who stole Piston. Was it really Piston? Had they been wrong?

"At least, we didn't set up the carnival in Boise."
He looked at the youngsters. What did they know?
The midget knew that Rossi had taken the burro
from a truck in Boise. Rossi had bragged about it.

"No, we didn't operate in Boise, but we passed
through there going from Salt Lake City to Spokane." he added.

"And could have stopped there for gas or food?"
Sara asked.

"Yes, we did." he answered.

"I knew it!" Christina shouted.

"Knew what?" The midget looked squarely at
her. "What are you kids up to?"

"Something wonderful!" she smiled. "Come on,
you guys." She had an idea and headed toward the
Ferris wheel.

She had an idea and headed toward the Ferris wheel.

Chapter 16.

CONFIRMING NEWS

"**O**h boy! We're back to riding rides!" Karen was happy when she thought the donkey business was over and done with.

Christina and Sara had not realized that everybody wasn't as interested in Piston as they were. After all, Piston had a bad reputation. Few people had ever said anything good about the poor guy. He had been a troublemaker. In fact, in Papa's area, the burro had been responsible for so much destruction, nobody wanted him around. They had been glad to see him loaded on that truck for Montana.

But, Christina and Sara were privileged to some information that the others knew nothing about.

In the last couple of years they had become aware of Mama and Little Prissy's ability to talk to each other. No one said anything about it, especially Papa.

105

But because this happens, Mama learns about everything going on in the animal kingdom on the farm.

It was a plain fact that Papa's animals all knew about Piston's reputation. The night of the storm, he kicked the barn apart and kicked poor old Mabel, injuring her so badly that she died. That was no secret. And there was Rosie. She still had a cast on her leg from his kicking fits. Rosie definitely harboured no love for this burro.

Perhaps if all of them could see him now, and see how badly he had been treated, their hearts would soften toward him. No one deserves beatings and starvation, not even a troublesome burro.

But Mama had learned of Mabel's dying words, her last wishes. Because of them, most of the animals had at least tried to forgive Piston.

Mabel had insisted before she died: "It was an accident. Piston didn't mean to hurt anyone. He was just afraid of the storm. When he's frightened, he kicks. Don't blame him, please. He's miserable enough the way it is."

From the looks of Piston now, he had fallen into the worst kind of luck. If anybody ever needed a friend, this poor fellow did.

Christina and Sara had been taught to be independent, to handle any situation, to make plans and follow through. What they were planning right now was pretty risky. But they had made up their minds, and heaven help anybody who might try to stop them.

They had chosen to take Kirk Locks into their confidence. He wasn't very surprised when they told him about Piston, who he was and where he had come from. Kirk checked a small notebook for the exact date that Vagabond Carnival Company would have been in Boise, Idaho. The date he had recorded matched the date Piston disappeared from the Mc-Mullen Brother's truck. From her purse, Christina pulled the newspaper clipping of the theft of Piston. It was crumpled and soiled but the date was there. The dates matched, perfectly.

Now they were sure. There was no doubt. Piston would have to be rescued from this madman Rossi, and it had to be done now, in the next few minutes.

Although the fair grounds would not close until ten o'clock, they had promised to meet Mama, Papa and Steven by the petting zoo, immediately after the close of the Roy Clark show. There was no time to waste.

"Danita, would you and Jenny take Karen to ride some more rides?" Christina asked. "She's afraid of Rossi, and besides, we don't want to get anybody into trouble. We kids," she nodded at Sara and Shawn, "can do what we have to do."

"Oh please, please," Karen pleaded.

Jenny wasn't sure, "Look, you guys, what are friends for? Let us help you."

"It's O.K.," Danita answered, "there isn't much time; you'd better get going. We'll take care of Karen, but we'll stay in this area. If you need us, we won't be very far away. O.K.?"

Christina and Sara knew they could count on their friends.

Danita, Jenny and Karen watched Christina, Sara and Shawn head back toward the turnstile. Thank goodness, a different fellow was there this time doing the hand stamping.

The trio scurried along the outside of the fence, never stopping until they were directly behind Rossi's trailer. There was no sound. Did that mean he was sleeping? If so, they were in luck. He could not harm them.

Kirk had watched as the group separated. His eyes followed the three going through the gate.

"Oh, no!" Kirk said to himself. "Be careful, kids!" For the moment, he could be of no help to them. The Ferris wheel was full; the lines were long. Every mother's child was attempting to ride as many rides as possible before closing time.

Whatever it was they were going to do, they would have to do it by themselves. What about Rossi? Was he really asleep?

Chapter 17

FREEDOM

At first, Christina, Sara and Shawn walked by Piston a couple of times. Piston wondered what was going on.

Many people were in the area, leaving the fair to get a head start on the mad dash for the parking lot. Cars were parked about a hundred feet away from Rossi's truck and trailer. It was not likely that anyone could see what the kids were doing, since there were other carnival trucks blocking the view.

The small trailer belonging to Rossi was behind and to the left of his truck. Where Piston was tied could be considered Rossi's front yard. The area was well lit from a tall pole light, except for one spot; the truck cast a big shadow over Piston, making it difficult to see how he was fastened.

"It's chain," Sara whispered. We'll never be able to break that!"

Shawn crawled around the side of the truck to get a better look. "There's got to be a snap somewhere, but I can't see it."

"We need a flashlight," Christina told them. "Or even a match."

Suddenly, the door of Rossi's trailer flew open. He flung it all the way back, banging the metal on the outside wall.

The kids scurried around to the side of the truck. They stuck together like syrup on hot pancakes.

Apparently, Rossi had not seen them. He staggered down the front stairs, taking a couple of steps in their direction. Then for no reason at all, he began yelling cuss words at Piston. Luckily, the obnoxious man stumbled to his knees. Plop! He fell on his face and lay motionless on the ground.

For a moment or two the kids backed off and waited, not knowing what to do. But Rossi did not move. They looked at him lying there like a dead log. The man had fallen just a few feet from where Piston was tied. Did they dare risk his waking?

"We can't give up now," Christina whispered. "Time is running out. I think we can outrun this old drunk if he decides to give us any trouble."

Shawn remembered the little flashlight on his bicycle lock keyring in his pocket. He fished it out and shined it on Piston's chains. There was a rusty looking snap that connected the tie chain to the one around his neck.

The girls, for once, were glad to have their brother along, if only for the use of the flashlight.

Rossi began to stir.

"As soon as we set him free, Shawn, take hold of the chain around his neck and lead him to grandpa's pick-up. I heard him tell you where he parked." Christina instructed. "Sara and I will follow along behind and help you load him."

Rossi was on his feet. He opened his eyes widely, trying to focus in on the kids. He began to growl. The sound seemed to come from the depths of the earth.

"Run!" someone shouted. But Christina continued working nervously on the stubborn, old, rusty snap. She looked up into Rossi's drunken face, aflame with anger. She was terrified, and with good reason.

Suddenly, the snap sprung open! Piston was free. Shawn made a quick grab for the chain around the burro's neck. But the confused animal moved his head. Shawn missed!

The staggering Rossi raised an empty, long necked bottle above his head. He intended to smash it over somebody's head. Christina was nearest.

Piston saw his chance to help. Before the intoxicated man could deliver the blow with the bottle, Piston, with all the strength and quickness he could muster, veered around behind his captor, turned and planted two hind feet firmly on Rossi's backsides.

The stinking old drunk went flying across the ground.

The stinking old drunk went flying across the ground.

Much later in the evening, he tried to pick himself up off the ground. But when he looked up, there was Kirk Locks, with a bull whip in his hand.

"Stay down, old man, or so help me I'll let you feel this leather across your back. Security talked to the police in Boise, Idaho. Seems like they are looking for someone who stole a burro."

Rossi did not try to get up.

Kirk hoped his young friends had been successful in getting the burro to safety. He stayed with Rossi until the police came to make the arrest. The midget watched. No longer was he silent. He laughed and visited with the policemen. Kirk told him that "Little Grey" was on his way home.

As for the kids, all six of them had met Mama, Papa and Steven at the appointed time and place. They were were giggling, but Mama and Papa paid no attention. Giggling was the normal state for this bunch.

"How was the show?" Karen asked.

"Great!" Papa answered, happy he didn't have to look all over the fairgrounds for the kids.

"Steven says we've got time for one more lemonade before the fair closes," Mama suggested.

"Someone is going to be riding home with you in the pickup, grandpa," Sara laughed, as they drank their drinks.

"Which one of you?" he asked.

The kids all laughed. Mama and Papa looked at each other, wondering if they had picked up more friends.

"I guess now is as good a time to tell them as any," Christina said.

"Well, you'd better tell us while we're walking to the car," Mama suggested. Some of the lights of the fair were being dimmed.

At first, everybody talked at once. But then they eased in to taking turns. At the end, they giggled about running through the parking lot with Piston. They thought someone would ask them where they were going with that burro. But no one did. After all, it's the State Fair. People were loading up animals all over the place. While they were heisting Piston, they were passed by a boy with two Nubean goats and a lady leading a Jersey cow.

"What's a burro or two among friends?" Shawn laughed.

If Mama had been around, she wouldn't have let them do it. Piston would have been taken away from Rossi all right, but not this way. These kids had really taken a chance. But before she could deliver the lecture she felt they had earned, Papa expressed his thoughts concerning the adventure. He looked at each one of them.

"I'm proud of you, all of you! I'll call the authorities first thing in the morning to make sure this

fellow, Rossi, doesn't get away with stealing and mis-
treating the Greystone's burro." Papa didn't know
that by morning, Rossi would be in jail. "Now, we've
got one more problem. One you kids didn't know
anything about. We can't take the burro to the Greystones. Glenn and Alice just moved to Phoenix. So?
Now? What are we going to do with that poor skinny
burro in the pickup?

Chapter 18.

ALL THE COMFORTS OF HOME

Piston slept in. Lazy golden sunbeams leaped through the east window of the big barn. Breakfast was ready any time the visitor wanted to eat. Alfalfa was piled high in the manger. A mixture of corn, oats and barley lined the feed box. Clean, fresh water sparkled in the metal tub and more wheat straw stood waiting to be used for a softer bed.

Papa had driven home carefully last night. He didn't want to put any more bumps and bruises on this already bumped and bruised animal. The big barn was the best spot for the new guest. It was quiet and peaceful, great for clearing one's mind and starting over.

Early in the day Mama called the vet. "Stop by the first chance you get, Mike, and have a look at Piston." He promised he would.

Before noon he had kept his promise. He and

116

Breakfast was ready for Piston

Papa gave Piston a thorough examination.

"It's hard to believe this is the same troublesome burro who left here a few weeks ago. I have never seen an animal more abused than this one. He's been underfed, overworked and beaten. I'll send off a report to Boise." From a good sized metal box, Mike located medicated soap and some healing spray for the bruises.

"What are you going to do with him?" he asked Papa.

Papa looked at Piston. "Let's get him well, Mike, and then we'll decide. My wife called Glenn and Alice this morning. They are certain to press charges against this Rossi character. For the time being, this young man will be our guest, and he's welcome."

Tom Cat was underfoot. He watched and listened, hanging on to every word. When he was sure he'd heard all there was to hear, he'd report first to Prissy and then spread the word. T.C. was the farm's walking newspaper. His proper name might as well be "The Informer".

As for Piston, his entire day was spent eating and sleeping. A time or two he ventured out to the lush pasture in the back of the barn. Once he stood and brayed for a couple of minutes. Off in the distance, somewhere on another farm, a burro was heard answering his call. Now and then, he glanced down at his legs, making sure the chains were gone. It was pitiful to see him do it.

The next day was Saturday. Mama left for Salem to pick up the grandkids. They were anxious to see Piston and the pigs.

Now that Piston had had a day of rest and relaxation, it was time to clean him up, to get rid of that horrible smell. Papa found a soft brush in the house. The burro was bathed with warm water and medicated soap. He enjoyed it so much that he kept dropping off to sleep. Once he nearly fell over on Papa. Papa laughed and put up his arm to stop the fall. Papa cleaned and scrubbed and cleaned, for an hour and a half.

The farrier came to trim Piston's hoofs. When he had gone, Papa sprayed the animal's cuts and bruises with the healing medication left by the vet.

Although Piston had a full stomach and smelled better than he had for weeks, he was a long way from being well.

"Give him time. He'll be o.k. now that he's with folks who know how to treat animals," the vet had said.

Papa watched as Piston limped out to the pasture. His heart went out to the poor fellow. Such a contrast to the healthy, ornery guy who had been loaded on that truck to Montana. Papa had forgiven Piston, just as Mabel did.

About the middle of the morning, a member of

the Boise, Idaho, police telephoned from Salem. Victor Rossi had been placed in his custody. Horse stealing charges awaited him in Idaho, certain to draw a stretch in prison. Also, there was the matter of his cruelty to animals. That crime may have been committed in several states. He would not get off easily. There would be more prison time and fines for Rossi to deal with.

The officer told Papa that several reliable witnesses had come forth. A midget fellow had been helpful. Rossi would have to pay for all the damages he did to the little man's trailer. Another fellow, Kirk Locks, had kept Rossi in line with a bull whip until Security got there. Kirk, the officer related, was anxious to know about the youngsters. Were they all right? Did they have any trouble getting the burro loaded?

Papa thought Kirk Locks to be a man of good heart and courage. He wanted to meet this man and to thank him, personally.

"You'll get another report from my vet," Papa told the officer. "We all want to help put this crazy Rossi away for a long time."

While the grandkids made their inspection tour, Little Prissy filled Mama in on all the news in the barn. Leeza had stopped worrying, now that she knew she got to keep her kittens. As soon as Leeza heard the news that her babies would not be sold, she moved them into an empty box in the storage room

Prissy paid T.C. a compliment.

of the farrowing barn. And now, there sat little Steven beside the box, naming the kittens. Leeza purred with pride and contentment.

The sows were excited about Piston being found and rescued; Patsy and Penny hoped he'd come and visit. Little Prissy told them she'd ask Mama.

There was more good news from Prissy ---about Rosie. Rosie was trying her hand at being nice. She hadn't had any practice, so it did not come easy.

Little Prissy always hoped Rosie might change. Rosie even asked Prissy about her babies. Tom Cat, who thought Rosie was rotten to the core, reluctantly admitted the sow had improved ---a little. Rosie's cast could be off in a few days.

Prissy paid T.C. a compliment. "Your kindness to Rosie worked wonders," she told him.

"And I think I handled it very well," he agreed. He had indeed handled it well. Such a cat!

Christina, Sara and Shawn were out in the pasture talking to Piston, arms around his neck, petting him.

Even before they began asking Papa if Piston could stay, they knew the answer, because they knew their grandfather.

"Anybody who went to the trouble you kids did to rescue an abused animal, deserves to keep him," Papa announced, just as they knew he would.

Mama looked at Steven sitting there by the cats. "We have Steven to thank. He saw a poor, lonely

Can we keep him?

little burro who looked hungry and he wanted to help. I'm sort of proud of my grandchildren," she told all of them.

"Me too!" Papa was grinning about something. "Now I think I'd like to go back to the fair, maybe Monday, and thank Kirk Locks, personally, I was wondering if anybody wants to go with me. Seems like you three got cheated out of riding rides."

Nobody said no!

At days' end, the girls ran through the barn "good-bying" the hogs.

A happy burro brayed a farewell ---for now---to the kids. They noticed he was walking with a quicker step. Papa saw it, too.

"Would you look at that donkey, Mama? He's gonna be just fine."

PIG OUT ON BOOKS!

How to order

If these items are not available in your local bookstore you may purchase them by ordering directly from the publisher. Mail your order, with your check or money order to: Jordan Valley Heritage House, 43592 Hwy. 226, Stayton, Oregon 97383.

Children's books by Colene Copeland
(ages 6 thru 11)

Priscilla (hc)	$8.95 plus $1.25 p&h per copy
Priscilla (pb)	$3.95 plus $1.00 p&h per copy
Little Prissy and T.C. (hc)	$8.95 plus $1.25 p&h per copy
Little Prissy and T.C. (pb)	$3.95 plus $1.00 p&h per copy
Piston and the Porkers (hc)	$8.95 plus $1.25 p&h per copy
Piston and the Porkers (pb)	$3.95 plus $1.00 p&h per copy

Priscilla poster 15 x 20, Priscilla says,
"Pig Out On Books!" $2.50 plus $1.00 p&h per copy

Priscilla Presentation -- Video tape (VHS or Beta) This is the author at school, telling her side of the Priscilla story, what it was really like to raise a pig in the house.

Very funny! $29.95 postage paid
                              rental -- $5.00 postage paid

Youth book by Christina M. McDade
(ages 10 thru 16)

Apples in the Sky (pb) $3.95 plus $1.00 p&h per copy

Thank you!   **postage credit issued